The Blonde With The Detachable Hand

Daz Eek

For Mom, who took me to my first library.

Note From Author

Please note, as an English author, it's only natural for me to use UK spellings rather than those of American English, like 'colour' instead of 'color', for example. I hope you enjoy the story!

Join Daz Eek's newsletter for news on future book releases at https://dazeek.blog/.

Contents

Lento

I t turned out, much to Brenda's surprise, what with it being so early in the morning that even the birds hadn't moved on from yawning to singing, that there was already a woman seated and waiting for the bus to the countryside. Not only that, but there was a fly seated and waiting, too. *Well*. You never know who you might come across, Brenda reminded herself.

The woman smiled at Brenda and courteously moved her bulging holdall from the bus shelter seating and onto her lap to make room for Brenda, who, in turn, returned the woman's smile and then sat down between the woman and the fly.

"Going somewhere nice?" the woman asked Brenda, as though she were an old and good friend and chatter about this, that, and the other was only natural and expected.

Brenda really didn't want a conversation with the woman, but she knew a question asked usually deserved an answer given. She wasn't an impolite person by nature. She tried to be a civil member of society, despite how it was for her nowadays. "An estate sale," she said.

"That *is* nice," the woman said, her face lighting up with interest.

In the silence that followed, Brenda sensed that the woman wanted to be asked the same question, as she saw the woman's lips twitching as though behind them there were a crowd of words, bustling and barging, frantic to be let out and heard by the closest person available. Once again, she succumbed to civility over rudeness. "What about you—going somewhere nice?"

"Me? I'm off to see my sister to take her a few things." She patted the holdall resting on her lap. "Her leg is acting up. So, if I'm being honest, I can't say it'll be nice—*no*."

"I'm sorry to hear that."

"Oh, I don't mind. It's good to have a day out. Nice or not. Besides, you've got to show him upstairs that you care about people with their bodily upsets, otherwise who's going to drop in on you when you have your own? Just yesterday, I felt a twinge in my own leg when I was putting the washing out. In my kneecap, it was. Our family has never had good legs. It's a curse. Are any of your body parts bothersome?"

Brenda kept her gloved hands, hands that, for anyone else, wouldn't have been gloved on such a warm summer's morning, motionless on her lap. "I'm okay."

"What I wouldn't do to be young again," the woman said. "Wait until you get to my age. That's when you find out one of your legs is going to play silly buggers. It's one big lottery, your body, isn't it? I've a friend, Rita's her name. She's seventy-nine. She lives five doors down from me. You know what she does? You'll never guess."

"I don't know," Brenda said.

"Go on, guess," the woman said.

Brenda reluctantly agreed to play the woman's guessing game. "She's seventy-nine?"

"Going on eighty," the woman said.

Brenda guessed. "She ballroom dances."

The woman laughed. "Wrong! She does triathlons! Swims, bikes, and runs. Miles and miles. Can you imagine? Seventy-nine, going on eighty, and doing triathlons! She always comes in last, but she does them triathlons, start to finish. She was in the paper not so long ago. They called her 'Super Gran.' She does her swimming training in the canal. You wouldn't get me in there, I'll tell you for nothing. I heard there's mutant fish in there that'll bite your fingers and toes off. That's what they say. I told Rita about the mutant fish. She told me to stop being daft. I told her, I'm not the one swimming in the canal with the mutant fish. How daft is that? I saw her the other night, down at the bingo. She did have all her fingers. I counted. I couldn't be sure of her toes being intact, not with those shoes she likes to wear. Like men's shoes, they are. She could kick in a door with those shoes."

Brenda noticed the woman staring at her hands. She kept them still as a dead mutant fish on a canalside bank.

The woman noticed Brenda noticing. "Don't mind me, I was just seeing if you had a ring on your finger, a pretty thing like you. But you're wearing those gloves. There's too much loneliness in the world for my liking. You see those types of things more when you get older. At least, I do. Ring, or not, I like to see two people together."

"No ring," Brenda said.

"Boyfriend?"

"No."

"Girlfriend?"

"No."

"Never mind. Won't be long before you're with someone, a pretty thing like you."

"We'll see."

"Your blonde hair—natural is it?"

"Yes," Brenda said, not minding the question, because if Liz was looking at her hair, she wasn't looking at her hands.

"I've always wished I was a natural blonde, like you are," Liz said. "It's a sin how much money I spent trying to pass myself off as a natural blonde when I was younger. It never worked. My hair didn't want to know." Again the woman looked at Brenda's hands. "Aren't you hot in those gloves? They said it's going to be baking today. Already is, if you ask me. We were all going to Spain for this kind of weather once. Now we're all staying at home with our Cornettos. They're nice gloves. Leather?"

"PVC."

"You don't say! I bought some PVC underwear once. At one of those parties. You know the ones. Never again! They rode up something awful. Well, don't catch heat stroke wearing those gloves. "

"I won't."

"I would. I'm not even wearing the underwear I like to put on in weather like this. But that's just between me and you." The woman looked down the road. "Ooh, look, here comes the bus. Early for once! Get yourself up. Now, you don't mind if I don't sit next to you? It's not that I'm being impolite, but I have this holdall and the bus at this time of day is always empty enough for taking two seats and spreading out."

"I don't mind."

"Oh, good. Well, I hope you find something nice at the estate sale. They have all types of stuff at things like that, don't they? If I wasn't going to see my sister with her leg, I might've come along with you. There might be a giraffe."

Brenda frowned. "A giraffe?"

"Not a real one, silly," Liz said, laughing. "A pottery or glass or plastic one. I collect giraffes. I don't know why. I just do. What are you looking for?"

"Music."

"Ooh, let me know if you find any Elvis. I love Elvis. 'Put Your Hand in the Hand' is my favourite. Not many Elvis fans would say that. But I'm an odd duck, people will tell you."

"Like Elvis?"

"Very much."

"I had a feeling you and I were going to get along when I first saw you. What's your name, by the way?"

"Brenda."

"Now there's a first. I've never met a Brenda before. You think I would've by now. It's a nice name. Suits you. I'm Liz."

"That's a nice name, too."

"It'll do."

The bus stopped at the bus shelter and Liz stepped on, humming her favourite Elvis song as she struggled with her holdall.

Brenda followed Liz onto the bus, hearing inside of her head Elvis singing the words to the song that Liz was humming. She knew how to play a lot of Elvis songs. What she didn't know was how to pay for her bus ride. Inside the bus, opposite the bus driver, she could see a machine. A machine that looked complicated and slightly threatening, as though it would have no qualms about snatching her hand off along with her bus fare. The last time she rode a bus there wasn't a machine. She studied how Liz paid for her bus ride. She didn't want it to appear that she wasn't keeping up with the times. She wanted to appear as an everyday person used to catching a bus, the kind of everyday person that caught the bus enough times to know how to properly pay their bus fare. She knew she'd be all thumbs when it came her turn, what with wearing gloves, what with her difficulties. And as she watched Liz paying her bus fare as easily as shaking a person's hand, she also happened to notice the fly from the bus shelter jump the queue, ahead of her, ahead of Liz, impatient to be on the bus, and she thought to herself that no one ever knows what a fly's next

Adagio

The bus took Brenda from the reds move will be—do they?and greys of the town to the greens and browns of the countryside. She looked out of the bus window and saw the trees and the hedgerows and the fields and agreed with Liz that it was always good to have a day out, give yourself a change of scenery. She hadn't been on a day out in a long time. She'd gotten to know more of what was happening behind her fridge on a cleaning day than what was happening beyond her front door every day of the week. She was glad that Liz had sat somewhere else. It wasn't as though she didn't like company. In fact, in the months she'd imprisoned herself inside of the four walls of her house, afraid to go out, there were times when company—someone with whom to have a chat, it didn't matter about what—was all that she craved. But today, being outside for the first time in a long time and having to speak to a person she'd never met before had become all a bit too much. She hoped Liz felt she'd given her the time of day, that she hadn't come off as being unfriendly. She looked down at her gloved hands. Liz was right: it would be too hot for gloves today. It was already too hot for gloves. Still, she wouldn't, *would never*, take those gloves off in public. Then, there came an unexpected buzzing and onto the bus window landed the fly from the bus shelter. She noticed the fly looking at her, and then perhaps at her gloved hands. That was okay. She expected the fly wouldn't have anything to say about her clothing choices—well, nothing she could understand, anyway. That made the fly just the right company. She could be on the bus sharing a window with the fly on a day out to the countryside.

***

Brenda saw the man gesturing for the bus to stop. Then, the man and his broken-down car were gone. She didn't feel sorry for the man being left behind. The bus driver was taking Liz, the fly, and her on their respective days out. She was going to the estate sale. Liz was going to see her sister. She didn't know where the fly was going, but she was sure that the fly didn't want to be late either. The bus driver knew that there hadn't been time to stop. She was glad to see the back of the man with the broken-down car. He'd looked like trouble that needed to be left at the side of the road.

***

Brenda heard a bell ring and then felt a tap on the shoulder. It was Liz.

"My stop is coming up," Liz said.

"Say hello to your sister for me," Brenda said. "I hope her leg gets better."

"That's nice of you. And good luck at the estate sale. Music, eh? Are you into LPs, tapes, or CDs?"

"Sheet music."

"What's that then?"

"It's printed music for playing."

"Ooh, what instrument do you play?"

"The chord organ."

"Like you see in a church?"

"No, it's a lot smaller and sounds a little different."

"Fancy that! Can you play Elvis on it?"

"You can play whatever you want."

"Well, I bet you play lovely. They put me on the xylophone at school, but my coordination wasn't up to it. When I wanted my left hand to go left it went right and when I wanted my right hand to go right it went left. The teacher took me off it soon enough. She said I was upsetting the other children with the sounds I was making."

The bus slowed and stopped for Liz to get off.

"Wouldn't it be grand if we were on the same bus coming back," Liz said. "I'll be on it before you if you can wrap your head round that. It's a strange route. If that happens, you can show me the sheet music you bought. And I can tell you about my sister's leg. How does that sound?"

"Sounds okay to me." Brenda said.

"Then it's a date," Liz said, smiling, pleased with the arrangement. "Let's both set our psychic clocks to be on the same bus going back."

Brenda watched Liz wrestle her holdall to the front of the bus. It was as though the holdall had a life of its own and didn't want any part in going to visit Liz's sister. She also saw the fly buzz after Liz and then settle upon the holdall, carried along. The fly obviously wasn't a fly for estate sales. It was a fly for visiting people, a fly for hearing the latest news, collecting people's stories, she imagined.

***

Brenda had read about the estate sale in the paper. It was a big advertisement for a big estate sale at a big house in the big countryside. When she'd read that there would be sheet music to buy her heart had fluttered with excitement. Then she'd thought about how she hadn't been out of the house in three months. Could she do it? And how would she get there? The estate sale was so far away from where she lived, and she no longer owned a car. What was the point of owning a car when she couldn't drive a car? But there would be a bus, wouldn't there? So, here she was—on a bus taking her to an estate sale to buy sheet music. She didn't play the chord organ like she used to play the chord organ, but she still liked to play despite how her playing sounded nowadays. She supposed it sounded like Liz playing the xylophone.

***

"In all my time driving this bus, nobody has ever got off at this stop," the bus driver said to Brenda. "Be safe. You never know who you might come across out in the middle of nowhere."

The bus driver's words weren't the words Brenda wanted to hear. Nevertheless, she'd travelled this far. Look what she'd accomplished! Here she was out of, and so very far away from, her little house. She really was on a day out, wasn't she? Who'd have thought it! She took a deep breath and stepped off the bus, out into the middle of nowhere, out into the big countryside. The estate sale was a mile or so away, and thankfully it was a straight walk without twists and turns for luring her in the wrong direction. She'd made sure to study the map the previous day. She knew where she was going. And of course, she'd walk fast, because the bus driver was correct—you never know who you might come across. Not just out in the middle of nowhere, but anywhere.

Adante

There wasn't a pavement for Brenda to walk along, only a verge of feathery grasses and rampant dandelions that separated wild flowery fields from the road. But that was fine. A day out was made for walking, wasn't it? When she was walking, she could think about her feet, and about how they worked in unison without ever a complaint, left and right and left and right, never out of step and time with each other, transporting her to wherever her heart fancied. She was glad that her feet remembered how to walk, how to behave. She hadn't been out walking since... She'd stopped going out walking. And when she was walking, she didn't have to think about her hands... her right hand. So, she'd think about her two good feet, left and right, and how they were walking her to the estate sale, left and right and left and right, and she'd think of what sheet music she'd find when she was at the estate sale. Perhaps she'd find some Elvis songs to play? She was young, but she knew Elvis and liked to play his songs. When Liz and she were together on the bus again, she could invite Liz over to her little house to hear her play 'Blue Suede Shoes' or 'Love Me Tender.' She'd the sheet music for those songs already. But then again—what on earth was she thinking? Surely, she was getting ahead of herself. She hadn't had a guest in her house since... Now, here she was planning on a get-together with somebody she hardly knew for an afternoon of Elvis songs played badly on the chord organ. It would be best for her to take baby steps, left and right and left and right, past fields of sweet-scented, candy-coloured flowers and morning-dewed grasses, making her day out, left and right and left and right, almost effortless. It felt good to her to do things effortlessly for a change. She'd forgotten how life could be like that sometimes—effortless. Still, she wouldn't amble and enjoy her new surroundings too much. Who would she come across? No one knew better than her what could come of that.

***

Brenda saw that her small house could fit into the monstrous house twenty times, thirty times, more. She knew her way around her own house blindfolded, downstairs and upstairs. But what about this house? Would she have to walk left, or walk right? Would she have to walk upstairs, or walk downstairs? Where would she find the sheet music that she was looking for? Perhaps she'd lose her way inside of the big house in the big countryside where even the people who lived there couldn't find their way to the kitchen without finding themselves in a broom closet. She walked up the winding driveway, longer than the street on which she lived, to the house. The gravel crunched beneath her feet, left and right and left and right. Ahead of her, there were a dozen or so cars parked in front of the house. First there'd been Liz, and now more people—would they want to talk to her as well? She hoped not. A van roared on by her spouting exhaust fumes, on the way to the estate sale too. The van with its four good wheels would reach the house before her with her two good feet, left and right and left and right. She hoped the driver wasn't looking to buy all of the sheet music at the sale. Where would that leave her? She should hurry along.

Allegretto

A man wearing a lanyard approached Brenda. "Hello, my name is Matthew. And if you don't mind me saying—you look lost."

"Hopelessly," Brenda said. She'd walked about the house looking in vain for what she'd come to buy. All the other people in the house appeared as though they knew where they were going, walking with purpose and knowledge. In contrast, she'd been walking in ever increasing amounts of desperation, a plaything of the house—which seemed, if it was possible, even bigger on the inside than it had looked from the outside. She was glad the man had recognised her as someone who needed assistance, even though it meant she'd have to speak to another new person.

Matthew gave Brenda the once over. "You're stamps, right?"

"Pardon?" Brenda said.

"Stamps are in Downstairs Room Twenty-Six, off Downstairs Hallway Three. You're currently in Downstairs Room Twelve, off Downstairs Hallway Five. If you want stamps, I'd hurry. There are already a couple of philatelists ahead of you. Last time I looked, they were like locusts in your veggie patch. You do have a map, don't you?"

Brenda shook her head.

"No map! Oh, you don't want to get lost in this place, dearie. This isn't the type of house for that type of going on. They're supposed to give you a map when you arrive. Without a map, we'd never see you again!"

"I just walked in," Brenda said, knowing that she'd purposefully circumnavigated two greeters, and their conversation, at the entrance to the house while they were preoccupied with handing out maps to other visitors.

Matthew shuddered so that the lanyard about his neck swung left and right, left and right like a person hanging. "I just walked in as well, and between you and me, I can't wait until I just walk out."

"I'm not stamps," Brenda said, attempting to refocus her helper on his job at hand: that of putting her on the right track to what she'd entered the house to buy. "I'm sheet music."

"Ah, sheet music!" Matthew said. "You know, that was going to be my first guess, but I couldn't see your hands with those gloves you're wearing, so I went with stamps."

Brenda hid her gloved hands behind her back. "I'm looking for sheet music."

"Yes, where are my manners! You haven't got all day, have you?" Matthew said. "So, sheet music—that'll be in Upstairs Room Six, down Upstairs Landing Six, off Upstairs Hallway Six. Want me to take you? I'm better than any map. Besides, what if you end up locked in a broom closet? Doors have a way of opening and closing under their own steam in this house."

***

Brenda hurried to keep up with her guide, her feet a blur, left and right and left and right. "We'll be there soon," Matthew had said, but he'd said that five minutes ago, his voice assured. Then, his voice had flipped into uncertainty when he'd said: "Yes, we'll be there soon. Upstairs Room Six, down Upstairs Landing Six, off Upstairs Hallway Six. That's where we'll find sheet music. That's where we're going—Upstairs Room Six, down Upstairs Landing Six, off Upstairs Hallway Six. And best to keep going, know where you're going, in this house. You never know who you may come across." What had Matthew meant when he'd said that? Where had she come to? Who might they come across? The other people in the house, people like her, looking to buy something, had dwindled away until it was now only herself, looking to buy sheet music, and Matthew leading the way, left and right and left and right. "Ah, look—here's Upstairs Hallway Six," Matthew eventually said, overwhelmingly relieved with his discovery. "Nearly there, yes, nearly there, thank goodness, we're nearly there."

***

The curtains were drawn in Room Six, down Upstairs Landing Six, off Upstairs Hallway Six. Brenda could see a person hiding in a shadowy corner of the big room in the big house in the big countryside. She watched Matthew march through the gloom to open the curtains as though in all of his life he'd never had a more important task to complete. As the curtains parted to reveal floor-to-ceiling gravestone windows, summer morning sunlight burst into the room to illuminate thousands of dust particles in the air, like so many ghostly flies. Brenda then, to her relief, saw that there wasn't a person hiding in the room after all; it was only a floor lamp over which had been thrown a white dust sheet.

"Here we are then," Matthew said, pointing to a large, round, and ornately-carved wooden table, "your sheet music."

Brenda saw that there was more sheet music than she thought there would be, more sheet music than she could ever afford to buy. "Thank you," she said. Whatever might she find that she would like to take home and play? Well, as best as she could play nowadays.

Matthew pulled out a small catalogue from his blazer pocket and flicked through its pages. "Sheet music. Sheet music. Yes, here we are, sheet music. Eight hundred and twenty five pieces of sheet music. Twenty pounds each."

Brenda thought of the money she'd brought with her to spend. "Twenty pounds?"

"You should've seen the prices of the items we sent to Sotheby's. It would frizz your hair," Matthew said. "I can't believe there are people who want to collect that sort of thing. There's a lot of them here today, too. *Marked*, they are. You need the eyes to see them, but when you're born a bit special, like my gran used to say, you can see them, all right. That's why I came over to you. I could see you were different from the rest of them." He laughed. "Hear me going on, and there's you wanting to get on with what you came here for. The family that's left wants to see the back of everything now they've seen the back of *him*. Who can blame them? I for one can't wait to see the back of this house. It was all touched by him, you know. Maybe that's why you're wearing those gloves, I don't know. I'll breathe easier when the day is over, I can tell you." He looked at his watch. "Five hours to go, good grief. Well, I'll leave you alone. You don't want me standing over you, getting in the way. Twenty pounds each then. Take whatever strikes your fancy and pay where you came in." He walked away from Brenda, but then he hesitated, stopped, and turned to face her once more. "Now you're sure you're going to be alright here, all alone? I can stay if you really want me to. I don't mind. Well, I do mind, if I'm telling the truth. They say it all went on in one of the upstairs rooms. Could've been this room! So just say the word, dearie, and I'll stay with you. The two of us together could deal with anything that might show up, couldn't we? We'd be heard. You should hear me scream when I see a spider. I can break glass, the notes I hit."

Brenda wondered what altogether was wrong with the house, about who had lived here and what had gone on—and who were these *marked* people? But what if finding out would frighten her from the room and out of the house? She would've come all this way for nothing. She'd have no new sheet music to play. She'd feel like a failure after summoning up the mettle needed to be here in the first place. No, she wouldn't be a little town mouse scared of the big house in the big countryside. She aimed to have a good day out, no matter what. "Don't worry about me. I'll be fine," she said, though when she said it, she knew that she was only being half truthful.

"Well, I hope you find something nice for yourself," Matthew said. "And because I like you, listen to this—there are no cameras watching you. And they won't be searching you when you leave. So, if you've got room beneath your jumper, if you know what I mean... nobody will ever know. Twenty pounds! Daylight robbery!"

On that, Matthew left Brenda alone in Room Six, down Upstairs Landing Six, off Upstairs Hallway Six with eight hundred and twenty five pieces of sheet music.

***

The selling of her car had provided Brenda with a decent amount of money to squirrel away, but after a year of living at home, never leaving home, without a job, that decent amount of money, spent on food and bills and house maintenance, had dwindled away to a pittance. But she deserved to treat herself, didn't she? It had been such a long time since she'd bought something for the fun of it, to bring a little joy into her life. She knew that the twenty pounds she'd brought with her to spend could go towards the groceries that she had delivered to her house, or keeping the electricity switched on—however, where was the joy in that? There was joy in buying sheet music on a day out. To most people it would seem a crushingly dull purchase, but to her, right now, buying a new piece of sheet music to play was right up there with buying a holiday to a far off, exotic location. Besides, she'd be able to find a job if she looked for one, couldn't she? She wasn't unemployable because she hadn't worked a job in a year. She could even find a job working from home, if she wanted. That would suit her. With a job like that, she could leave her house whenever it felt right to leave the house, like it had felt right to leave the house that morning. Yes, spending twenty pounds on sheet music wasn't all that extravagant when soon she'd be working again, topping up that pittance. Still, the slightly odd, but likeable nevertheless, Matthew had been right—twenty pounds! What a lot to pay! She'd hoped she could buy more than one piece of sheet music, but that would have to be her lot. Of course, there was his not-so-subtle suggestion of taking what she wanted without paying, hidden beneath her jumper, but that didn't sound like something she could carry through. When was it she'd ever stolen anything? *Never*, was the answer. Besides, she knew she wasn't the type to get away with things. She's once been reprimanded by a police officer—who'd seemingly sprung out of nowhere—for not using a pedestrian crossing to get to the other side of the road. And everybody did that without a slap on the hand! No—to entertain Matthew's tip would simply lead to her being caught red-handed and red-faced.

She looked about the room and strangely didn't see a piano, or any musical instrument for that matter. Had they been sold at the Sotheby's auction Matthew had spoken about? If this had been a music room, Room Six, down Upstairs Landing Six, off Upstairs Hallway Six, then what a grand music room it must've been, with its spaciousness and high ceilings and the view through the windows to the trees and green fields beyond. She played her chord organ in a cramped corner of her living room facing a wall that she'd painted sky blue and upon which she'd hung pictures of trees and green fields. Of course there was no comparison, but in that small space she'd fashioned for herself, she could escape and be happy for a while, even upon hearing all of the wrong notes she'd play, though lately when she played, the happiness she experienced was becoming less and less, replaced more and more by thoughts of...

But she wouldn't think of that—she was on a day out! She'd come to buy sheet music, and if she could only buy one piece of sheet music, well, even that would be lovely. She reached into her shoulder bag, and then took out and opened her purse. Her twenty pound note wasn't there. She suddenly felt hot all over. She'd absolutely left the house with the money. She'd seen it on the bus, wrapped beneath the five pound note for her bus fare. Her face flamed crimson remembering when she'd paid for her bus ride, unsure of what to do, fumbling with her purse, the gloves she was wearing, her right hand—her bad hand—making what should've been the easiest task in the world, paying for a simple bus ride, absurdly difficult to accomplish. What had she gone and done? She'd dropped her twenty pound note on the bus, hadn't she? It was the only explanation.

Brenda pulled out a chair from beneath the table and slumped down onto the seat in despair. She felt like she'd never get up again. There she'd stay, frozen in time, for someone to come along and cover her with a white dust sheet. She'd become the person hiding in the big room in the big house in the big countryside. *You never know who you might come across.* What a failure she was! A flash of anger overwhelmed her, and she struck out at one of the tall stacks of sheet music laid out on the table, which wobbled and then tumbled over, scattering sheet music everywhere. She shot up from the chair, clasping her right gloved hand, the offending hand, her *bad hand*, to her mouth. Look at what she'd done! She wanted to run and keep on running, running from Room Six, down Upstairs Landing Six, off Upstairs Hallway Six, running from the big house in the big countryside to the bus that would come and return her back home. She should never have come out today! What a fool she'd been to think that she could have a nice day out! Now she should go and forget she'd ever left her little house for the big house in the big countryside. Yet she couldn't leave the room as it was now—messy. She had to put matters right, leave the sheet music as she'd found it, in a neatly stacked pile. What would Matthew think of her if she were to leave the jumble of sheet music not put right? He'd likely have second thoughts about her being one of those *marked* people he'd told her about, whatever he'd meant by that.

Brenda began to corral the fallen sheet music, neatly stacking another pile rising up from the table, one piece of sheet music at a time. As she did so, she examined some of the sheet music closely as things of particular interest caught her eye—a beautifully inked cover, a decorative font. All of the sheet music was old, possibly centuries old, but despite that there were few to no creases or edge tears to mar any page. Whomever had owned the sheet music had been a careful and considerate collector. And, sorely regretting her outburst, her vandalism, she'd now be one too, imagining that as the sheet music passed from her hands, left and right, that *Danse macabre*, composer Charles-Camille Saint-Saëns, or *Fantasiaquasi Sonata*, composer Franz Liszt, or *Caprice No. 13*, composer Niccolò Paganini, belonged to her, and were hers to play. Surprisingly, she thought of Liz. This wasn't a sheet music sale for finding Elvis. If she still had her twenty pounds, she'd have been buying sheet music the likes of which she'd never bought before. Her sheet music collection were songs from the fifties, which most people might've found strange given her age. But those songs spoke to her, called to her, in a way that songs written afterwards, and during her lifetime, never did speak to her, call to her. Was she an old soul? And when she played those songs she always played from the sheet music, even though she knew those songs off by heart. So, she'd always place the sheet music for *All I Have To Do Is Dream*, say, on the music rack of her chord organ and turn the pages of the sheet music, with her left hand, her good hand, as she played. When she did that, it was as if the Everly Brothers were in the room with her, that they'd become as one through the notes written down on the page, the music being played, or as well as she could play those notes nowadays. She liked to think that the Everly Brothers didn't mind the way she played the chord organ nowadays. *You have found me!* She snapped out of her reverie. Of course, the sheet music didn't say that, but still it was speaking to her, calling to her, wasn't it?

You have found me, and I am yours! As she held this new piece of sheet music, Brenda felt an electric tingling in the fingers of both hands, left and right, good and bad, a sensation that travelled up from her hands and then into her arms and it was such a surprise, a shock, that she dropped the sheet music onto the table. From that distance, a safe distance, she saw the sheet music was titled: *En Djävuls Hämnd,*

Sammansatt av Abernus Åkesson, Sigtuna, 1792S. The language was Scandinavian, wasn't it? Norwegian? Finnish? Swedish perhaps? The word 'helande' looked familiar to her, as though she may have seen it written down before, heard the word spoken before—maybe on her TV when she'd watched a night of subtitled Ingmar Bergman movies? Was that it? Well, she'd know more about the sheet music after she took it home with her and could investigate. Where had that thought come from! What was she thinking! Why would she want to take this sheet music home? And even if she wanted to do that—how would she pay for it? But it had to be hers, it *wanted* to be hers! Even now, there on the table, the sheet music continued to speak to her, call out to her. *You have found me, and I am yours!* A staggering need surged through her to have the sheet music back in her hands, left and right, for it to be hers for always. But how could she make that happen when she'd no money? Would they set the sheet music aside for her, so she could come back later and pay the twenty pounds? No, that wouldn't work. This was a one-day only estate sale. She'd never be able to make it back home and then back to the house in time, especially without a car. Besides, two days out in one day was out of the question! She supposed she could give her address for the sheet music to be mailed to her, after which she'd then mail the twenty pounds to complete the sale. As if the people running the estate sale would go through all of that palaver, trust her to be true to her word! A thought then came to Brenda, an unscrupulous thought that had been planted inside of her head by Matthew, her guide, a thought that had now seeded and quickly bloomed as the only option available to her given the present circumstances. What would be the loss of one piece of sheet music, one twenty pound note, when there'd be so many more pieces of sheet music left for others to buy, so much money to be collected? What harm would a little thievery do? She'd been shown Room Six, down

Upstairs Landing Six, off Upstairs Hallway Six, and had been told nobody would see, nobody would check for, a piece of sheet music hidden beneath her jumper. As if hearing her thoughts, the sheet music spoke to her, called out to her once more: *I've always been yours. No other's.* She reached out and tentatively touched the sheet music with her right hand, her bad hand, and again felt the electric tingling pass through her wretched and hidden fingers. It was a feeling that felt both wrong and unnatural and yet right and natural at the same time. She had to have the sheet music! The sheet music wanted her to have it! And who else would ever want it as much as her? Who else would give it a good home, take care of it as though *she'd* written the music herself, slaved over every quarter note, half note, semiquaver, quaver—not the composer, Abernus Åkesson? She picked up the sheet music and the electric tingling spread throughout the whole of her body, and she'd never felt so alive, and also, as well—how could she describe it?—so close to death? And she knew that feeling well. She'd experienced death, the man, drifting her out in a boat towards a horizon of never-ending darkness. It was a feeling that lived with her every day, both awake and asleep. People had said she should try to move on. She should try to heal. That she shouldn't allow what had happened to consume her whole being, define her as a person. But what did those people know other than their textbook talk that didn't help her? What did they know of what would *really* help her? What she craved, what was never offered to her as a means of moving on, of healing—was *revenge!* Was that so much to ask for? Yes, it was revenge that, more and more, occupied her thoughts while she played song after song on her chord organ. Why shouldn't she think of revenge on her day out! And back in her little house, she'd think of it when she played *En Djävuls Hämnd*. Her shoulder bag would be too small for this new sheet music, *her* sheet music now, to fit inside, but beneath her jumper would, as Matthew had mentioned, be a perfect hiding place.

On her way out of the room, Brenda happened to see, by coincidence or fate, she didn't know which, a tiny ceramic giraffe all by itself atop a beautifully made bureau. She knew someone who collected giraffes. And, unlike her sheet music, it would fit conveniently inside of her shoulder bag. So, she took that, too. "In for a penny," she said to herself.

***

Brenda walked along upstairs hallway after upstairs hallway, left and right and left and right, and found herself back where she started—outside of Room Six, down Upstairs Landing Six, off Upstairs Hallway Six. She set off again, and found herself within another part of the upstairs of the house, without a stairway to take her downstairs. From there, she started out in a different direction and still she couldn't find the stairway that had brought her upstairs to take her back downstairs. Did the stairway still exist? She could hear the faint voices of people talking in the downstairs of the house, going here and going there, knowing where they were going, and she wanted to be one of them; she wanted to be free of the house altogether. Should she shout for someone to come and rescue her from her entrapment? If she did, would anyone even hear? But she was a thief, wasn't she? Surely whoever came to rescue her would recognise her thievery. Her theft was likely written all over her face. She'd be at the police station before tea time. Did they send people to prison for stealing sheet music? She would keep quiet, keep herself to herself, a poor fly caught in a hungry spider's web. She deserved to be eaten up by the spider, by the house, didn't she? She shouldn't have been foolish enough to think that she could get away with her larceny. And her comeuppance would be just—to never leave the big house in the big countryside, to be trapped upstairs for all eternity. Here she would remain until she died and maybe one day someone would find her and say to her desiccated body... *Where did you come from?* Why, she'd come on a day out to buy sheet music. That's how it had all started. She wished she was safe and sound back in her little house. Usually on a Saturday about this time, she'd be playing her chord organ—playing from sheet music that she'd bought, not stolen. She liked those songs, she should've been happy with playing those songs only. Why did she think her life could be improved with new sheet music to play? It was such a little thing. How could it make such a big difference in her life? She never should've gone on a day out. Nobody knew that she'd come on a day out, except Liz. Who'd report her as missing if she was unable to leave the house?

"Get ahold of yourself, Brenda," she said to herself. "You're being ridiculous." Of course she'd be able to leave the house. She should calm down. She'd worked herself up into a state for no reason at all. What a ninny she was! She was only in a house, no different to hers when she thought about it, a house with a downstairs and an upstairs, a house with rooms and hallways and landings, exactly like her house had rooms and hallways and landings, only her little house had fewer, is all. Sooner or later, she'd find her way downstairs, and then she'd be free. Her two good feet wouldn't let her down, they knew what they were doing, left and right and left and right.

Brenda reached the end of a hallway and came to a door. There she stood, contemplating whether the door would be a helpful door. She hadn't come across this particular door, carved with worrying faces, up until now, she was sure of it. It *could* be a helpful door, a door to be opened, a door beyond which there would be a stairway to take her downstairs. She opened the door and stepped into a large, dark room. Even in the darkness, she could see there was no stairway. Then, a voice from within the room shouted, "Close the door behind you!"

Brenda flinched at the barking command, and instinctively moved to do as she'd been told, but she saw the door was already closed. Matthew had said to her that the doors in the house seemed to have a life of their own, opening and closing at will. Now, there she stood locked up within the room with its darkness and shadows and another person, and then she saw there was a second stranger in the room, too, and also a third, a fourth, and all four of them were sitting about a round table with their hands, left and right and left and right, laid on the table in front of them, each person's hand touching the hand of the person sitting opposite. The four strange people looked at her.

"Petulia, finally!" one of them said, a woman, her voice recognisable to Brenda as the one who had told her to close the door, her tone now considerably more annoyed. "We started without you. We couldn't wait all day. Now hurry along and come and join us."

Brenda stood still, confused. She wasn't Petulia.

"Don't just stand there like a ghost," the annoyed woman said. "If they find us here before we're finished, you'll be to blame. You don't want that, do you?"

"I was looking for a way out," Brenda said.

The annoyed woman, noting Brenda's unfamiliar voice, said, "You're not Petulia."

Brenda gave herself up by revealing her name.

"Brenda? We don't know any Brenda."

"There's a Bernice," one of the other three, a bald man, said. "Perhaps she said her name was Bernice."

"She said her name was Brenda," the annoyed woman said. "Besides, Bernice is a brunette. And she's a blonde now I can see her better."

"Well, she looks like Bernice from where I'm sitting," the bald man said.

"That may well be," the annoyed woman said, glaring at the bald man. "But she said her name was Brenda, and she has blonde hair. You remember the time you had hair, don't you? So, it can't be Bernice, can it?"

"I'll just shut up then," the bald man said.

"There's a blessing," the annoyed woman said. She turned her attention back to Brenda. "Now it's not what you think. We all just wanted a sit-down. Parvati here is seventy-three. And her legs aren't what they used to be."

"I'm seventy-three, and my legs aren't what they used to be," Parvati said.

"It is what she thinks," the bald man said, not shutting up after all. "What else could it be? We're all going to prison."

"We're not going to prison," the annoyed woman said. "They don't send you to prison for having a nice sit-down."

"But we're not having a nice sit-down," the bald man said.

"They don't send you to prison for having a séance either," the annoyed woman said. Then, having quickly reflected upon what she'd just proclaimed, she said, "I meant to say, of course, a nice sit-down. Not séance. "

"Some séance this is," said the last of the four to speak, a man wearing a fedora hat. "We're getting nowhere fast."

"We would be if it weren't for Petulia being late and now this interruption," the annoyed woman said.

"I'll be going now, if you don't mind," Brenda said. Were these the *marked* people Matthew had been talking about? If there were, she didn't want to be hanging about any longer than needs be. *You never know who might come across.*

"And where will you be going?" the annoyed woman asked.

"She's going to the police," the bald man said.

"I'm seventy-three and my legs aren't what they used to be," Parvati said.

"I could be at home watching the match," the man wearing the fedora said. "Yet here I am trying to contact the recently departed."

The annoyed woman turned on the man wearing the fedora. "Be quiet," she said. "You don't have to let the whole world know our business."

The four strangers noticed Brenda backing away from them, towards the door.

"What's that sticking out from beneath your jumper?" the annoyed woman asked Brenda.

Brenda looked down and saw the sheet music, her secret, peeping out from beneath her jumper.

She pushed the sheet music back up into its hiding place. "Nothing," she said.

"It was a recording device," the bald man said. "We're all doomed."

"I'm seventy-three and my legs aren't what they used to be," Parvati said. "Oh, let her go," the man wearing the fedora said, "it's plain to see that she's no interest in us. And I don't blame her. We're a shambles. We deserve to be locked up for crimes against the dark arts."

It was a remark that drove the four people into a bout of squabbling, and Brenda, seeing an opportunity to flee the room, did so post-haste, though not before struggling with the door, which didn't want to open, but which eventually, with fervent rattling of the handle, did so—much to her relief.

Outside of the room, she heard Parvati—was it?—shout, "He's here! Look!" After which, she heard the man wearing the fedora—was it?—comment, "That's a bloody hat stand, woman!" After which, she heard the bald man—was it?—say, "No, look—*beyond* the hat stand!" Then she heard the annoyed woman—it had to be her—exclaim, "Oh, Master!"

"There you are," came a familiar voice then. "I've been looking for you all over."

Brenda turned to see Matthew approaching. She'd never been so relieved to see someone in her life.

"Lost again, I see," Matthew said. He pointed to the door she'd just come out of. "That's Room Nineteen, off Upstairs Hallway Five, that is. You don't want to end up there, believe me. Now let's get you downstairs and on your way." He looked at his watch. "And I won't be long behind you. Won't that be a moment in my life!"

***

A left and a right and a left and a right, and Matthew had led Brenda to a stairway leading downstairs.

At the top of the stairs, Matthew said to Brenda, "If you don't mind me saying, your sheet music is showing."

Brenda corrected the matter, blushing as red as her jumper.

"Not to worry. Your secret's safe with me, dearie," Matthew said, taking Brenda's right hand, her *bad hand*, in his left hand, leading her down the stairs. When he did so, he cringed as though he'd suddenly taken hold of something disagreeable. Though, if that were the case, he was too polite to comment, or unlock his hand from Brenda's.

On their way down the stairs, Brenda hesitated slightly and then carried on as though she hadn't recognised the man coming up the stairs. He looked as angry as the last time she'd seen him. He was the man who'd been stranded at the side of the road with his broken down car. He was breathing heavily and sweat sheened his face. The man looked at her and then at Matthew, taking notice of the lanyard and badge that Matthew wore around his neck.

"Are you working here?" the man asked Matthew.

"Not for much longer, if I can help it," Matthew said.

"I'm looking for the sheet music you have listed for sale."

"Everyone's after sheet music today."

The man's eyes narrowed, like a snake's eyes. "What do you mean?"

Brenda squeezed Matthew's hand. For some reason, she didn't want the man knowing that she'd come to buy sheet music, too. The man didn't look quite right to her. There was something off about him.

Matthew caught on. "Sheets, you say? Yes, there's a lot of people looking for sheets today. I wouldn't buy second hand sheets, but that's just me. You don't know who slept beneath them, do you? Somebody could've died beneath secondhand sheets. I couldn't have that in my head going to bed. I wouldn't sleep a wink."

The man wiped his sweaty face with a handkerchief. "I didn't say sheets. I said sheet music. I'm looking for sheet music."

Matthew laughed. "Oh, sheet music! I thought you said sheets. It's been a long day. Sheet music, sheet music, sheet music. Yes, if memory serves, you'll find sheet music in Room Five, down Upstairs Landing Four, off Upstairs Hallway Three. You have a map, don't you?"

"They didn't have any left. I'm late. Do you have one?" the man asked.

"Sorry. I gave mine away," Matthew said, lying.

The man looked at his watch. "Can you show me? You're closing soon."

"I can't. Sorry. I'm dealing with this young lady, you see. First come, first served. I'm sure you'll understand."

Brenda looked down at the stairway carpet, so she didn't have to look at the man now looking at her. The carpet was a deep purple and there were tiny red devilish faces woven into the fabric that were looking at her while she was looking at them. She didn't like to think so but she saw lips moving, speaking to her.

"Never mind," said the man, frustrated. "I'll find the room myself."

It was then that the sheet music that Brenda had been hiding dropped from beneath her jumper to the deep purple carpet with the devilish faces. She thought she saw the devils laughing at the mishap.

"What's that?" the man asked.

Brenda let go of Matthew's hand and quickly picked up the sheet music and stuffed it back up beneath her jumper. With her right hand, her *bad hand*, she held the sheet music in place. Once again, she felt that electric tingling.

"What's it to you?" Matthew asked the man.

"Looked like sheet music to me," the man said.

Matthew turned to Brenda. "Was it sheet music?"

Brenda shook her head.

"There you are," Matthew said, "it wasn't sheet music."

"It looked like it to me," the man said.

"Well, we'll never know," Matthew said. "Now if you don't mind, the young lady and I have places to be." He turned to Brenda. "Don't we, dearie?"

Brenda nodded.

The man, for his part, huffed and applied his sodden handkerchief to his sweaty face.

"Room Eleven, down Upstairs Landing Two, off Upstairs Hallway Three, that's where you'll find sheet music," Matthew said to the man, again lying through his teeth. "Hurry now, we're shutting shop on the hour, same for those who were early as those who were late."

With that, Brenda and Matthew carried on downstairs, leaving the man behind muttering expletives.

"He's one of them," Matthew said to Brenda. "*Marked* up and down, he is. I spoke to another not so long ago. Petulia was her name. She's on a wild goose chase, too. You've got to have your fun, try and make it a day out, don't you?"

Allegro

"**B**londie," the man said from inside of the car, the driver's window wound down, "can you show me something?"

Brenda continued walking, ignoring the man. The bus driver hadn't stopped for the man to get on the bus, and she wouldn't stop for the man to show him something. She'd nothing to show that she wanted him to see. She looked at her watch. The bus would be arriving at the stop farther down the road in five minutes. But buses were always late, weren't they? No. This bus, Liz's and her bus, not the man's bus, would arrive on time.

"Come on, Blondie, I only want you to show me something. Where's the harm in that?" The words the man used filled Brenda with a well-known terror. She'd lived this day before, but this man wasn't that man. Then how did he know those words, those words that haunted her day and night—*Blondie, can you show me something?* How could that be?

"Why won't you look at me," the man said. "Why won't you talk to me? It's not what you think. I just want you to show me something. Then I'll leave you alone. I promise."

Brenda knew the man wouldn't leave her alone, she knew that his words were lies. The man who wasn't this man had promised her the same thing, and he hadn't left her alone. She'd keep on walking, not looking, not speaking, keep on walking with her two good feet, left and right and left and right. She could see the bus stop ahead of her, there wasn't much farther to walk. When she reached the bus stop, the bus would arrive on time, not late, with Liz on it, and maybe the fly, too. On the bus, she'd be safe. The man couldn't get to her when she was on the bus. She belonged on the bus, and the man didn't belong. But what if the bus *was* late? And what if the bus was on time, even? Would on time be too late? She again looked at her watch. There were still four minutes before the bus was supposed to arrive. How would she keep the man from her for a whole four minutes? A lot could happen in that time. She knew that better than most people.

"It wasn't at the auction like it was supposed to be," the man said. "So I thought to myself, where else could it be? That's what brought me to that estate sale. But it wasn't there either. *You* were at the estate sale though, weren't you? Tell me—do you play music well?"

Brenda thought back to the days when she used to play music well, back before she met the man who wasn't this man. She didn't play music well anymore. But she still liked to play. The sheet music was hers, finders keepers. She wouldn't show him the *something* he wanted to see. He could get lost.

"You can always tell a good pianist by their hands, but you're wearing gloves," the man said.

"Why are you wearing gloves? A bit hot for gloves, isn't it? What's under your gloves? What are you hiding from me, from everyone? I know what you're hiding under your jumper. Show me, Blondie."

It was then that Brenda heard the man's car begin to cough and splutter, and the man swore. And then the car was behind her, out of sight. She heard a car door slam.

"Where are you going, Blondie? Come to me and show me something."

Brenda started to run. She wouldn't look back, and if she didn't look back she'd never know how near or far the man was, near to having her, far from having her, and she'd run, run away from the big house in the big countryside and away from the man and away from the bus stop, because the bus *wouldn't* be on time, and she'd never stop running until she was safe and sound inside of her little house, she'd two good feet, left and right and left and right. And as she ran, she held her sheet music tight in place, beneath her jumper, with her left hand, her one good hand. She wouldn't show, the man wouldn't have it, not for as long as there was a breath in her body, as the sheet music was hers, she'd come to get it on a day out. No. She wouldn't live the day that she'd lived once before all over again. Then with a roar, wheels passed her, wheels that weren't late or on time, big bus wheels that were *early*, wheels on a bus going round and round, faster than her feet, left and right and left and right, and then slower than her feet, left and right and left and right. The bus wanted her to catch up, she was going to catch up. The bus driver wouldn't let the man onto the bus, like he hadn't earlier. The bus was an early bus for meeting her if she was early enough, running fast enough, left and right and left and right, not for meeting the man. She wouldn't show him anything.

***

"You never know who you might come across, right?" Liz said, having made a point of it this time to sit next to Brenda on the bus, her formerly stuffed-to-bursting holdall now flattened on her lap.

"How's your sister?" Brenda asked. She didn't want to talk anymore about what had happened. She was on a bus, moving on. And she wanted Liz to move on with her, away from the big house in the big countryside. Away from the man. She'd had her day out. Now she was going home.

"Oh, there was a fly she didn't care for, but all told she'll live. It was on her Eccles cake, the fly, disguised as a current," Liz said.

Brenda gasped. "She ate the fly?"

"Good lord, no! Imagine eating a fly thinking it was a current and then tasting it wasn't a current," Liz said. "It would be enough to put you off Eccles cakes for life. Is it a current or is it a fly, you'd always be thinking. I tried to get it with the newspaper, but it was too fast for me. That's a fly for you." She placed a hand on Brenda's right hand, her bad hand. Then she removed that same hand, as though she'd touched something not quite right. "You should tell the police about him."

"It's done with," Brenda said. She then looked about the bus for the fly. She'd left for the big house in the big house countryside with Liz and the fly, and she wanted to return from the big house in the big countryside with Liz and the fly.

"What about the next poor woman?"

"That's not what he wanted."

"It's what they all want."

Then came a fly, landing on Liz's holdall. Brenda immediately recognised the fly. They'd spent time together. It was a town fly that had been on a day out to the countryside. A fly for visiting Liz's sister. Now, it was a fly to her rescue, a fly to end Liz's conversation about the man.

"That looks like my sister's fly," Liz said.

"I'm sure it isn't," Brenda said. She didn't want Liz to renew her battle with the fly. She wondered if Liz had a newspaper in her holdall.

"It *is* my sister's fly. Look, there's a bit of Eccles cake on it."

Brenda, too, saw the bit of Eccles cake stuck to the fly.

"I'll take cherry bakewells next time. You can spot a fly on a cherry bakewell."

Brenda watched Liz shoo the fly away with her hand, the fly landing on the seat across the aisle, opposite herself. She was glad Liz didn't have a newspaper.

"Now what were we talking about? Oh yes—"

Brenda quickly pulled out the sheet music that was still hidden beneath her jumper. "Do you want to see what I got at the sale?" She showed Liz the sheet music. Again came the electric tingling as she handled the sheet music.

"No Elvis, then?" Liz asked.

"They didn't have any Elvis," Brenda said.

"That's a shame. But so long as you're happy with what you've got."

"I am."

"What are those symbols about?" Liz asked, pointing at the peculiar shapes that bordered the front page of the sheet music.

"I don't know," Brenda said. "But I like them."

"They give me the fidgets. I saw a Peter Cushing film once at the old Odeon, before they closed it down and made it a bingo hall. That had symbols like those in it. Carved into a gravestone they were. I hid behind my hands the most of that film. Good job my hands are the size of oven mitts. Foreign music, is it? I can't read any of the words on it."

"Swedish, I think."

"Them ABBA were Swedish, weren't they? Is it ABBA?"

"No, it's classical, by the looks of it."

"See, you're an odd duck, too."

"It spoke to me."

"What did it say?"

"I'm not sure."

"I don't know Swedish either."

Brenda looked out of the bus window. The greens and browns of the countryside had been replaced with the reds and greys of the town. She saw the shops and the houses and the people and thought about when would be the next time she'd have a day out. Perhaps, for the near future, it would be best to stay at home, in her little house. She looked at the fly resting on the seat across the aisle. The fly seemed to be nodding that this decision was a good one.

"Oh, I nearly forgot," Liz said, "The driver and I think you dropped this." Liz then gave Brenda a twenty pound note. "And even if it isn't yours, after the day you've had it should be yours."

"Thank you," Brenda said. "And I nearly forgot, too. This is for you." She reached into her shoulder bag and took out her other stolen item. She gave it to Liz.

"A giraffe! I love it! Thank you!"

"It wanted to be with you, not on its own in that big, old house.."

"Well, it can come home with me all right. Say, you should look me up one day and we can both listen to Elvis. I'm 62 Urmston Road. You'll find me."

"I'd like that," Brenda said, knowing she'd probably never visit Liz. After all, who would she meet on the way there, the way back?

Vivace

"Here we are," Brenda said to the fly. "It's not much, but it's mine." Once off the bus, the fly had followed her home. It was a visiting fly, after all.

Brenda ushered the fly into her little house. She felt relieved to be back home. Here, she knew that she wouldn't inadvertently shut herself in a broom closet. She knew what she would come across. The fly buzzed about her, taking in its new surroundings. She wouldn't tell the fly that she'd killed other flies that had come into her house. She wouldn't own up to keeping a can of fly spray, not a newspaper, in the cupboard beneath the kitchen sink. On the matter of her tiny murders, she'd remain quiet. The fly could be with her, and she could be with the fly. After all, she wanted to be a good host and a good host didn't murder their invited guests, flies or otherwise.

Brenda removed her gloves, left and right, and placed them on the hallway side table beside the front door, next to where she'd put her precious sheet music. She soothed some of the pain in her right hand with her left hand. Inside of her little house, her home, there was no need to hide any part of her, from her hair down to her toenails. She didn't mind showing her hands to the fly. She was sure the fly had seen other things that were worse than what she could ever show. When you were small and had wings and could go anywhere you pleased, like a fly, you got to see all sorts, from the beautiful to the horrific.

"This is my left hand," Brenda said to the fly, showing her good hand. "And this is my right hand," she said, showing her bad hand. "You might get used to it, and you might not." She stood there in front of the fly, with both of her hands, left and right, laid out in front of her as though she were a child showing a parent their hands were clean enough to be allowed to eat dinner. She watched as the fly buzzed about her left hand and then her right hand, her hand that didn't look like a hand. She'd been right. The fly wasn't shaken by the one part of her body that was an abomination to a human being's eyes. If only people reacted to her deformity as the fly! She'd bought the gloves to wear because she knew people wouldn't react to her in the same way as a fly would. People would see her, her bad hand, and then they'd look away in disgust as though she were a living, walking monster, or perhaps alternatively, they'd look at her with ghoulish fascination, pointing at her, studying her, asking her questions that had no right to be asked. Would Liz have been one of those people? The bus driver? Estate-sale Matthew? The man? Today she'd masqueraded as someone plain and normal when she knew she wasn't plain and normal at all. But that was okay, wasn't it? After all, doesn't everyone masquerade in one way or another each day of their lives?

"I'm hungry," she said to the fly. "Are you?"

The fly buzzed at a higher pitch, which Brenda took to mean that the fly had an appetite, too.

"I don't have any Eccles cakes," Brenda said. "I hope you don't mind."

The fly circled about her, which Brenda took to mean that the fly didn't mind there would be no Eccles cakes for dinner.

"Okay, let's see what we can cook up," Brenda said, and the fly followed Brenda to the kitchen.

As they went, Brenda wondered if she should use both of her hands to eat, a fork and a knife in either, seeming as though she'd company. Usually, by herself, she only ate using her left hand, her good hand, alternating between a fork, knife, or a spoon, the choice of eating utensil depending on the meal. Born right-handed, she was proud of how she'd mastered command over her left hand—nowadays it did as it was told, when it was told, which was a whole lot more than could be said for her right hand. And when she and the fly sat down to eat, the topic of dinner conversation would be her new sheet music. She was excited to sit down at her chord organ and play music that her ears had never heard before, even though she knew the music she'd hear wouldn't be pretty. But that didn't matter—it had been a long time since she'd come across a piece of excitement in her life, and so she'd hold onto that feeling for as long as she could.

Presto

"This is where I play," Brenda said to the fly, leading it to the corner of her living room where her chord organ sat on a small table, just the right height for her to sit down on a wooden chair and play all the songs she cared to play. Brenda watched as the fly buzzed about her blue-sky wall and pictures of trees and fields hung above the vintage chord organ that she'd bought for a steal at a car boot sale, those times when she used to have regular days out, when she never worried who she might come across.

"Would you like to hear me play?" Brenda asked the fly. It was only polite to ask, wasn't it? Perhaps the fly that didn't like music? She didn't want to subject her guest to something they didn't like. Maybe the fly would rather watch what was on the TV? Or perhaps she could put on one of her Dr. Who DVDs? Had the fly ever seen a Cyberman or a Sea Devil?

The fly settled atop her new sheet music, and Brenda took that as a sign that the fly would like to hear her play.

"I don't play like I used to play," Brenda said, "but I try." She sat down at the chord organ, suddenly nervous. She'd never played music for someone else before, certainly not a fly. She'd only ever played for her own enjoyment. On the TV, she'd watched pianists play for large audiences, and she'd wondered how they ever drummed up the nerve to perform with all those eyes and ears waiting to be entertained. Now it was her turn. But not only that, she was about to play music that was written in 1792, music with which she wasn't familiar. This only added to her nervousness. Would the composition be too far beyond her capability to play nowadays? How on earth would her sick and twisted excuse for a right hand cope, keep up, with the notes waiting to be played, so many of them, complexly placed, parading along the sheet music's upper stave? The fly landed on that hand. If it hadn't been *this* fly she would've shooed the fly away, not knowing where it had been, what it had been doing. She would've gone to get the fly spray that she kept in the cupboard beneath the kitchen sink. She would've killed the fly. At that moment, she felt sorry for all the flies she'd previously murdered. Didn't flies only live for a short while—a month?—and there she'd been putting an end to their already short lives. Perhaps she'd murdered one of this fly's relatives? If she had, she was sorry. "I'm sorry," she said to the fly. The fly looked at her, and she looked at the fly. Was that forgiveness she saw in its red dot eyes? If it was, she was thankful to the fly. She knew how hard it was to forgive. She'd been told that to help in her recovery, she should forgive. But she would never forgive the man, that monstrous man, for destroying her right hand, a hand that no surgeon could ever put right. She'd take herself to her grave unforgivingly. And if that meant she couldn't move on from her trauma, so be it. She'd stay in her little house, not moving on, because she knew that you never know who you might come across and those kinds of people didn't deserve forgiveness; they weren't *people* in any shape or form. The fly hopped up and down upon the hand that had been ruthlessly given her, and she took that to mean that she should get on with playing already. So, she placed her fingers on the chord organ's keys, took a deep breath, and began to play her new sheet music...

En Djävuls Hämnd
Sammansatt av Abernus Åkesson
Sigtuna, 1792S

... Brenda's hands, left and right, moved across the chord organ's keys, white and black and white and black, and once again there came the now-familiar electric tingling rising up through her fingers, her hands, her arms, the whole of her body, and the music that soared from the chord organ to fill her living room from floor to ceiling was music the likes of which she'd never heard before, quarter notes, half notes, semiquavers, quavers that she wanted to shut her ears to, stop playing—what a sick and twisted mind that had conjured such a devilish sound, for her, only her, to come across and play!—but for all of that, she was compelled to play more, hear more, and as she played, out of the music came a voice, strong and forceful, calling out to her, speaking to her: *You may say my mind my is sick and twisted for writing this music, for giving it to you, but look and see how your sick and twisted hand now plays, left and right and left and right, all because of me; yes, it was meant to be that you came across me, and I came across you—yes, look and see how that sick and twisted hand of yours now plays!* And it was true. She saw! But it couldn't be. And yet it was! There was her right hand, her *bad hand*, free of her... horribly... grotesquely—*detached!* That sick and twisted hand of hers, now oozing, dripping blood, moving across the keys of her chord organ, white and black and red and white and black and red, a freakish creature crawled up from the darkest depths of the ocean, and playing masterfully, without the assistance of her right arm, which hung limply at her side—and it played in a way that it had never played, even when it was a hand that was usable, that *belonged* to her, and as the hand played, she saw upon it the fly, dancing from one bent finger to the next, merry to the music it was hearing, and then abruptly, the fly fluttered upwards to the sheet music to turn a new page for her to play. And then again came the voice she knew to be that of the composer Abernus Akesson, calling out to her, a voice rich with experiential pleasure, saying: *Shall I show you something else? There—do you see? You never know who might come across. Isn't that true... Blondie?* And, yes, she did see herself—and what accursed sorcery made it so that she could see?—transported back in time and place to the park to be again joined with the man who had made her hand a monster's hand, yes, *you never know who you might come across*, and she didn't want to see, be there, live through that day again, but all the same she was there, she *did* see, and even with eyes closed she still saw—*how?*—and through all of this she continued to play her music, couldn't stop playing, without now the need to pay attention to the sheet music that she was playing, for now she was each and every note, and each and every note was her, with her hands, good and bad, normal and abnormal, magicked along the keyboard, left and right and left and right, white and black and red and white and black and red, as if strung above the chord organ's keys—marionettes for performing, left and right and left and right, white and black red and white and black and red, orchestrated by the diabolical Abernus Åkesson and his music, yes, there she was and there was the man, yes, she *did* see. *Blondie*, he said to her as she walked on by, *can you show me something?* No, she wouldn't show the man anything. She didn't know him, and she didn't like the look of him either. She'd only come out to the park because it was such a lovely summer's afternoon, and she wanted to see the blue sky and smell the green grass. It wasn't a visit to the countryside, but it felt good to be on a little day out. But where were the other people? Shouldn't there be lovers holding hands? A person and their dog on a walk? A child running free at last from their parents? All of them, like her, wanting to enjoy a little day out in the park? Why was there only the man she'd come across? *Wait up, Blondie*, the man in the park said to her, he was behind her now, his voice louder, irritated. *I only want you to show me something. Come on, give me the time of day, Blondie. Then I'll leave you alone. I promise.* She didn't believe the man would leave her alone even if she showed him whatever he wanted to see, and she didn't have anything to show the man, not now, not ever. She wouldn't show. She'd keep on walking, her feet taking her away from the man, left and right and left and right, and if she didn't look behind her, the man couldn't be there, was he? It was only her in the park, and soon she'd be back home in her little house, out of the rain that was now beginning to fall. Maybe the lovers, the person and their dog, the child and their parents, had heard about the rain coming and decided to stay at home in their own little houses? They'd left her alone with the man, but she was the only person in the park, the man wasn't in the park with her—*was he?*—behind her, calling out to her. *I'm not going anywhere, Blondie, so come on, show me what I want to see,* the man said to her, his voice now defiant, commanding. And the rain that now fell had tiny, urgent hands pushing her out of the park, back to her little house, ushering her to trade her walking feet for running feet, left and right and left and right. Yes, she'd run, run faster than she'd ever run, and she wouldn't look behind her, because if she didn't look behind her the man wasn't there, he wasn't now running, too, like her, and maybe he'd give up on her if she ran fast enough, she'd two good feet, left and right and left and right, faster than the man's two good feet, and she never saw the fly, there in her little living room in her little house, wing its way into the air, joyous for all that was happening, but she saw, felt, the man's hands upon her—his feet had run faster than her feet in the park after all, left and right and left and right—hands that shoved her, sent her tumbling to the ground, the wet grass, and she looked up at the man in the park, and he looked down upon her, he'd a face her eyes shut from seeing, a face, even for that brief moment, she'd never forget, she knew it would always be tattooed onto her mind. *All I wanted was for you to show me something, Blondie. That's all*, the man in the park said. *Was that so much to ask? Now here we are. You and me. Me and you. So come on, show me something. Show me the time of day, Blondie. See, I see you have the time.* She'd bought the watch from a charity shop because it reminded her of the watch her mom used to wear and she could afford it, and it had always kept good time, but it hadn't told her it was a bad time to go walking in the park, and she couldn't stop the man from stomping on her right hand with his shoes for kicking doors down, over and over and over, breaking her watch, she could hear its workings fracturing, falling to bits and pieces, breaking her right hand, she could hear its workings fracturing too, and she heard the man in the park say, *You never know who you might come across. Isn't that right, Blondie?* And she tried to move her hand away from the man's stomping feet, left and right and left and right, but the man's feet were faster than her right hand, until it was pointless trying to move that hand, because it felt as though she didn't have a right hand at all, that it had gone missing, fled from all the pain, that it was detached. Then, suddenly, she wasn't in the park with the man, she was outside of a pub, and the fly was with her, buzzing about her, too. It was a pub she knew, a pub in her little town, a pub she'd never been inside of before, a pub that had been in the papers for all the wrong reasons, she knew the music she was playing, Abernus Åkesson, had taken her there, and she looked through the pub's rain-soaked window and she saw the man from the park, the man who'd destroyed her life, her hand, it a face she'd never forget. There he was sitting by himself in a corner of the pub, and there she was standing outside, and she slammed her right hand onto the pub's wet window, a bloodied and sick and twisted hand, as though she might shove the man to the ground as he'd shoved her to the ground, and for once she felt that hand free of pain, a pain that made everything she did so difficult, at times impossible, but she did all she could, as best she could, all the same; she'd picked herself up from the ground, the wet grass, and carried on, as the man had carried on, and there he was, inside of the pub, and here she was, outside of the pub, and somewhere in the distance, through the streets and over the houses, she heard music playing, a devilish music, and Abernus Åkesson, the composer of that song that was only hers to play, said: *Yes, there he is, and here you are. You never know who you might come across. Play so you will both meet again. Play!* She played, she was not herself, she was a woman possessed.

***

"Show me something," Archie Broadbent said, looking into his empty pint glass, divining the beer foam shapes clinging to the sides of the glass, waiting for a vision to come to him. "Come on, give me the time of day."

Things hadn't gone well for him in London, and so, without too much thinking on the matter, he'd come home, back to his old stomping grounds. That's not to say Birmingham, the town he'd sprung up from, had ever treated him any better than London. But at least now he felt *fitted* into his surroundings, as though he'd slipped his feet, left and right, into an old and comfortable pair of shoes. Was it safe for him to be here? He didn't care—the city was *his* again! Now the streets that he walked held him as one of their own instead of as a stranger. Now he knew where he could fill his belly with the best curries outside of India. And, thankfully, there were pubs like this one, where there was still a cheap pint to be had and the clientele weren't the kind of down South flash people he'd rather shove screaming into early graves. But that music! That *unholy* music! Where was it coming from? The jukebox was smashed in and not working. And he'd asked the tasty barmaid if she could hear what he was hearing—music not fit for human ears to hear!—and she'd looked at him as though he'd a packet of screws loose. He'd had to restrain himself from using his fist to wipe that pitying look from her pretty face. That wouldn't have done. He didn't want the few other people in the pub describing him to the police and for the police to then put two and two together, associating himself with some of his other historical indiscretions about town, if they could count that high. Never mind, he'd see Florence—that's what others in the pub had called her—after last calls, when it was dark and quiet, when it was just the two of them, and then he wouldn't spare the rod in instructing her on how to treat one of her new regulars with proper respect.

"Show me something," Archie said again, still looking into his empty pint glass. It was his ninth beer drunk that night. The first eight he'd polished off throughout the evening hadn't shown him anything to entertain his singular interests, but this beer finished—the ninth—was at last beginning to tell him a story worthy of his predilections. A story that was only for his divining, no one else's. It had always been that way. He supposed he could say that he was what?... *marked?*... yes, *marked*, to be able to see such things with his eyes, left and right, and if he was—bless the god who had looked down upon him and bestowed such a charitable gift. For there, as he interpreted the mysteries of the foam slowly sloughing down the curved insides of the beer glass, he began to see a second, different, pretty face of the night taking shape, a face that he remembered well. How could he ever forget the likeness of one of his conquests? Each one of them hung inside of his memory like so many portraits lovingly collected for his private viewing. Yes, it was *her*. You never know who you might come across. "Hello, Blondie," he said. "Here to show me something more?"

What a nice day out in the park that was! He'd been shown through his vision that she'd be there walking alone, through looking down into the glass of a sixth pint drunk, there for him to add to his gallery of conquests. Their meeting had been a whole lot of fun, *his* type of fun. And a day out was meant to be fun. Now here she was being shown to him once more. To meet again? He'd like that. She'd been one of his favourites. "Yes, Blondie, show me something *more* with you," he said, looking into his pint glass. But that music! How was he supposed to give himself over to what he was seeing with that bloody music playing! And though once the music that he heard was irritatingly soft, as though it were coming from somewhere outside of the pub, from afar, through the streets and over the houses, to visit him, now that same music was becoming louder, deafening, as though it were being played by some fiend inside of the pub. There were only two other people in the pub with him now, and they got on as though they couldn't hear what he was hearing. It seemed a noiseless, music-free Saturday night out for them.

"Hey, you pair," Archie shouted over at two men playing a game of dominoes two tables away, "do you hear that music?"

The two men looked up from their game with its black-spotted white tiles laid down on the table, left and right and left and right.

"Music, you say?" one said.

"I don't hear any music," the other said. "Do you?" he asked his competitor.

"Not me," came the reply.

"You two are having me on," Archie said.

The two men went back to playing their dominoes.

"Pay no attention to him," one said.

"We'll both be better off for that," the other said.

"If I say there's music, there's bleeding well music, and don't tell me any different!" Archie slammed his empty beer glass upon the table. There *was* music playing! He could hear it! And if *he* could hear it, why weren't the two old duffers, the barmaid, hearing it too? Why were they lying to him? He put his hands to his ears in an attempt to block out the sound, but it was an exercise in futility. If anything, the music was louder! He looked into his empty pint glass. "Come back to me, Blondie," he said. "Show me something." But his vision had changed, reshaped, from the last time he'd looked. His careless handling of the beer glass had altered everything! How stupid he'd been! What was it that he now saw—a hand? Yes, a hand. No, not just a hand but—a *detached* hand? A sick and twisted and bloodied hand! Where had Blondie gone? He wanted her back! He wrapped both of his hands around the empty glass as though it were a woman's neck, and looked harder. His Blondie was still nowhere to be seen. She had escaped him. Yet the image of the hand remained there in the glass, sculpted in foam. And were those sick and twisted and bloodied fingers now *lengthening*, reaching out to him, up the insides of the glass? What did this new vision mean? And how was he meant to interpret it, with the distraction of that hellish music playing!

It was then that Archie saw a fly land atop the rim of his beer glass. A fly from nowhere. He looked at the fly, and the fly looked at him. Was the fly smiling? Ridiculous. A fly couldn't smile. But this fly did look like it was smiling—at *him*! It wasn't a pleasant smile, either. It was more of a smug smile, like the fly knew something that he didn't know. But he was the one with the gift of knowing *everything and all*, not the fly. He could drink a beer and then look inside of the empty glass and know more than a simple, shit-eating fly. He asked the fly, "So what could you know that I don't?" He watched the fly take to the air, gone as fast as it had appeared, seemingly dancing to the music as it went.

***

Brenda was far off, back through streets and over houses, still sitting at her chord organ inside of her little house, but the woman with the red hair saw her standing outside of the pub.

"Coming in?" the woman asked Brenda.

Brenda shook her head.

"Suit yourself," the woman said, entering the pub.

Brenda watched as that which wasn't part of her, but *was* part of her, crept into the pub behind the woman.

Unseen.

***

We are brother and sister, sister and brother, comrades in arms, they are left and I am right, and together we have touched and recoiled, held and dropped, pushed away and taken in, broken and mended, found and lost—we have played music together! *And when once, to your eyes, you may have seen us as the same, reflections of each other, left and right, I am now nothing but a crawling terror, something for your eyes to look away from, something that shouldn't be, but has come to be—still, lend me your eyes, left and right,* look, *and let me show you something—the vengeance that will be mine, given to me to take justly, through loud and glorious music played, for only him to hear!*

***

"I bought you a pint," the woman with the red hair said. "Like some company?"

Archie looked up from his empty pint glass, his face a tempest. The music, the fly, and now this woman—would the interruptions plaguing him never end? He stared at the woman and then at the pint of beer and then back at the woman. He didn't care for women with red hair, even those offering him a free drink. He preferred women with blonde hair. He wanted Blondie, not this poor, red-haired substitute. "Piss off if you know what's good for you," he said.

"Suit yourself," the woman with the red hair said, and she walked back to the bar.

***

From egg to larva to pupa to a fly on the wall. Have you ever wanted to be a fly on the wall?—to not be seen and yet see all things? Oh, the stories I could tell sprung from what I have seen! And I have dined sumptuously on these stories with my eyes, left and right, as I have dined on the sweetest of flower nectar and the savoriness of the dead. Stories that would majestically decorate both the walls of heaven and hell. And what of this story that I see, here a fly on this wall? How will this story end on this my last day, part of a world, which you solipsistically call yours? Yes, death, delicious death, has something to show all of us, both fly and you. This man that I see... You never know who, or what, you might come across, do you know?

***

"Pay no attention to him," Florence said, her hand in a packet of salt and vinegar crisps, "and we'll all be better off." It was her first night serving behind the bar, and already she was regretting taking the job. What you had to put up with these days to earn a few more pence! Were the free crisps worth it?

The woman with the red hair agreed with the barmaid's way of thinking about the man sitting alone in the corner of the pub, mummering at his empty pint glass. She'd preferred the blonde standing outside, anyway. She was more up her street. Perhaps she'd show herself?

***

The blonde with the detachable hand watched as that which wasn't hers, but *was* hers, crept along the pub floor, trailing smudged lines of blood as it made its way underneath the table at which the man sat muttering to himself, looking deeply into an empty beer glass. She lived every moment of the hand's existence. She felt the cold, rough wood floor beneath palm and fingertips, the electric tingling of excited anticipation for what was to come. She felt the man's shoe, there under the table, a shoe for stomping on a hand. And she heard the music that she, another self, through streets and over houses, feverishly played—*En Djävuls Hämnd...* A Devil's Revenge! Finally, she knew all, she understood why the music had wanted her, had to be hers, was hers only.

***

Once, in one of the cheaper digs where he'd had the misfortune of spending the night, Archie had awoken to a large black rat creeping up his right leg, over ankle and onto calf, and what he felt now—it felt a lot like *that* time, as if that same rat had found his same leg. He hurriedly looked beneath the table, and his eyes, looking left and right, saw not a rat, but a *hand*—a bloodied and sick and twisted *hand*. A hand creeping over his knee and onto his thigh and then over his crotch. It was the hand that he'd seen inside of his beer glass. A detached hand! A hand with a life of its own—*alive,* outside of his vision. A hand now creeping up over his chest. His disbelief gave way to the reality of what was happening. He took his own two hands, left and right, to the devilish hand that was upon him, using the buttons of his shirt like the steps of a ladder to climb higher, yet higher, dripping blood from a wrist that had long said goodbye to the arm to which it was once attached. But the hand would not release him, smothering his own two hands with hot, crimson blood—it was a hand with the strength of a hundred hands. And the music, that awful music, which seemingly only he could hear, burnt and blistered his ears, as the hand found a home about his neck, squeezing tightly, a vice—and then began to twist, left and right and left and right. He stood up, kicking the table away from him, struggling with the hand as his breath was taken away from him, his screams silenced. Surely someone saw, someone would come to help?

But the two men playing dominoes only looked at each other. "Pay no attention to him," one said to the other.

And, "Pay no attention to him," Florence said to the woman with the red hair.

As for Archie, with his eyesight fading, blackening, his final vision was of a blonde standing outside of the pub, looking in at him through a window. No matter what, she'd always be his Blondie.

Slutet

Grave

B renda knelt at the bottom of her back garden and, inside of an ordinary round tin that once held a selection of chocolates for Christmas eating, she carefully and lovingly placed the fly upon a bedding of honey-fragranced dandelion flowers that she'd picked from her lawn. She then arranged five freshly baked Eccles cakes about the fly, star-like. She'd never baked Eccles cakes before, and she hoped the fly wouldn't be disappointed with her efforts. Finally, she laid *En Djävuls Hämnd*—once only for her, now only for the fly—over all. Everything as it should be, she fixed the lid back in place, then lowered the fly's tin casket—no longer ordinary, but precious—into a hole she'd dug with her hands, left and right, good and bad, and covered it with earth wetted with her tears and shone upon with her smile. It had been a visiting fly, a fly for collecting people's stories, she'd been right. Her story, for better or worse, had been the last story ever shown to the fly. The fly, like her, understood that you never know who you might come across. Perhaps, after all, she'd look up Liz for an afternoon of Elvis…?

End

Also by Daz Eek

Daz Eek is also the author of *The Crows That Ate Sunday*, *Two Knocks For Arthur*, and *Ottilie's Obituary & Other Horror Stories*.

Join Daz Eek's newsletter for news on future book releases at https://dazeek.blog/.